C000182054

Zoë d'Ay

PATRICK AND THE CAT
WHO SAW BEYOND TIME

BOOKS

Winchester, UK
New York, USA

PATRICK AND THE CAT
WHO SAW BEYOND TIME

Copyright © 2004 O Books
46A West Street, Alresford, Hants SO24 9AU, U.K.
Tel: +44 (0) 1962 736880 Fax: +44 (0) 1962 736881
E-mail: office@johnhunt-publishing.com
www.johnhunt-publishing.com
www.0-books.net

U.S. office:
240 West 35th Street, Suite 500
New York, NY10001
E-mail: obooks@aol.com

Text: © 2004 Zoë d'Ay
Illustrations: © 2004 Zoë d'Ay

Design: Graham Whiteman Design

ISBN 1 903816 72 6

A CIP catalogue record for this book is available from the British Library.

Printed by Tien Wah Press, Singapore.

CONTENTS

ACKNOWLEDGMENTS

My deep thanks to Carol, a Koori from Wollongong, for sharing with me the beautiful poem by Hyllus Maris which I have included in the text; also to Hyemeyohsts Storm for his story of Little Mouse from "Seven Arrows".

Zoë d'Ay
November 2003

FOREWORD

This is a magical story. It is about a cat and a boy and a family in the Australian Bush. But it is a magical cat and a magical boy and a magical country. The cat comes from beyond time and teaches the boy to discover the hidden mystery of his own soul and of the land on which he lives. We all live in two worlds. There is the world of everyday life and there is the world of dreams and fantasy and poetry and also of religion. It is a strange world which can lead to madness but can also lead to the Ultimate Truth.

The cat whose name is Om, the sacred word which opens the door of the unconscious, teaches the boy to go deep into his inner self and to find there the secret of his existence, the hidden mystery which lies at the heart of life. He discovers there not only his own myth, his life story, but also the myth of the Aboriginal people of Australia, the myth of the land and its inhabitants, its forests and mountains and streams, its birds and animals and its human beings, which still underlies the surface of Australian life. But deeper than this, the cat takes the boy back to Bethlehem and Calvary, to the mystery of death and resurrection which underlies all human history and all human life.

But the story is not merely about these things. It is in itself a myth, a sacred story, which opens the heart to the other world, which lies beyond and yet within this everyday world. It is itself an initiation into that inner mystery.

The illustrations, which are in the form of mandalas, further this impression of magic and mystery. They are truly inspired. They appear like the work of an accomplished artist, but in reality are the spontaneous expressions of an inspired imagination.

Bede Griffiths OSB
Saccidananda Ashram
Shantivanam
Tannirpalli - 639107
Kulittalai, Tiruchi Dt.
Tamil Nadu 1986

DEDICATION

This story came from a dream I had at the time of my meeting with Father Bede Griffiths OSB, on his first visit to Australia in 1985. I was known then as Swami Sitadevi Saraswati, and Father Bede had requested to be taken to the ashram at Mangrove Mountain to which I belonged. I was blessed to be his chaperone for three days. The imagery in the dream was of the Boy, and a Cat, a "Silver Moon Cat who saw beyond Time." A year later, having responded to Father Bede's invitation to visit his ashram in India, the story was born without conscious plan or direction. The end of the story was a deeply moving experience for me and led to my becoming an Oblate of the Benedictine Ashram of which Father Bede was Acharya. It was he who illuminated for me the Christian mystery of the Resurrection and I was received into the Catholic Church at Ealing Abbey in London shortly after.

During the few weeks in which the story was unfolding I was in London sitting with Mrs. Irina Tweedie, a Sufi and a Saint. It was her presence that activated the pictorial visions of the mandalas accompanying the story. I have never painted in my life, nor had any formal drawing lessons. I can only say they came from Somewhere Else. Ignoring the rational, logical knowledge that said I could not paint, and that I was afraid to even try, I gave my unconscious space by going into silence each Tuesday. After a short meditation I would simply sit quietly and wait to hear the dialogue between the heart holding the vision and the hand holding the paintbrush. It was as if "I" was a silent witness. Later I learnt this was a traditional way of all spiritual painting from the Greek and Russian icon painters to the Tibetan masters of Thangka. The paintings you see are exactly as they came.

I dedicate the story to Father Bede and the mandalas to Mrs. Tweedie in recognition of my humble gratitude to both great spiritual guides of my own inner journey.

Zoë d'Ay
Glastonbury 2003

ILLUSTRATIONS

INTRODUCTION

We are all searching for our own myth, our way of being, the path that will take us to the Sacred Mountains. Very often we turn to other peoples' myths because in the West we have relegated myth to fairytale instead of understanding that myths and symbols are archetypes buried deep within every human being and are the key to show us the way to our own inner kingdom: the kingdom within, where God dwells. Yet even the word "God" is part of a myth, just as are the Sacred Mountains or the Dreamtime. The Transcendent Reality is always beyond the words we can give it – and the experience is beyond words for those who travel the inner way.

This is the story of a small boy who could not find his own myth, could not find his Sacred Mountain, although his heart told him of its Reality. It wasn't until he had been taken through his Dreamdoors to explore the Creation myths of other people that he found his own.

Apart from the boy – who in any case is the eternal child within each of us – everything in the story is real. The Silver Moon Cat left me three years ago. He was my companion for fifteen years, and because he became blind when he was very,

very young I was his outer eyes while he taught me to see with my inner eye, gave me "in" sight. He was the pass for me to go through my own Dreamdoors. If he should come to you – please let me know, so that I can thank him properly for his gifts to me.

Sitadevi
Springbrook 1986

CHAPTER ONE

ONCE THERE WAS A SOUND…

Love knew it was the first seed of the soul. It had lain silent since before time was Time, before eagles had learnt to fly, and before the flannel flowers had learnt to blossom; before the sea moaned and before the snow had learnt to melt. There was no night then, and no day, there was darkness hidden in darkness and all was formless. The One in whom Love was to be born breathed in its own power, in infinite peace, and only the One was. A single breath of the One was 4,321,000 years, and civilizations rose and fell in the time of that single breath – but even before that, the One – was.

It breathed: the sound of its breath was Silence and the vibration of the Silence was Sound. The Sound of Silence. A Hum, a vast Hum, much greater than space. The Hum went on through eternity and could be heard, perceived, when the earth was still and the heart at peace. O-o-o-m-m-m. On and on, contracting and expanding: Om, Om, Om. There was no break in the eternal sound; the break seemed to be there because human minds and thoughts interrupted its ceaseless rhythm.

When love arose in the breath of the One the formless chaos, swirling and eddying, exploded into flame; the flame of Love burnt for seven days and for seven nights and, as the fire cooled, the formless chaos that was burnt, blistered and cracked and separated and formed whole planets and stars. And the earth in its birth swung like a moth around the sun whose burning was as old as the Dreaming, as old as the Humming of the Breath of the One before Time.

The Dreaming was held as a secret in a corner of the earth. The land that held it had also lain silent, waiting for the People. And the People who came were from a land as ancient as itself and the color of the soil; they knew and understood how to move to the sacred rhythm of life. Once there had

The flame of Love ··· formed whole planets and stars

been other lands on this earth whose people had known the secret of the earth's Dreaming and its Birth, and they too had moved with the rhythm of the earth's breathing; they too had taken only what they had needed from the earth's great store, but now they had gone and their secrets were hidden.

CHAPTER TWO

AND THEN THERE WAS A BOY...

Somewhere on this ancient land a Boy sat in his classroom, the end of his pen resting on his lower lip and his eyes staring out of the window at nothing in particular, but his ears were taking in the sound of the bush around him. The classroom was the whole school, and there were eleven children sitting in there with him whose ages spanned the primary school years of five to twelve. He was ten and a half. There was one teacher, a man as craggy and as weathered as the tabletop escarpment where the children lived, three thousand feet up in the misty rainforest mountain of Springbrook, behind the Gold Coast. The "Green behind the Gold" the real estate developers called it. Luckily there were not too many amenities on the mountain and so it only attracted the people who loved its mists and its austerity and its solitude. The Boy had lived here a year now, his family had moved because their doctor had advised them the clear air of the mountains, any mountain, may help the boy's tiredness. His family had looked for such a mountain for a long time, and had come from a long way, from Adelaide, many thousands of miles south and west. The Boy insisted on one thing only: that the family cat come with them.

He was diligent about his school work and today, because the other children had gone on a walk that would prove too strenuous for him on the return climb up the steep forest track, the Boy had asked to stay behind while he finished a drawing he had begun last week. He was quite alone in the room.

CHAPTER THREE

AND IN BETWEEN THERE WAS A CAT...

When the One had breathed, before Time, a particle of moondust, a moondrop, silvery white with a bluish tinge, smoky blue and radiant and cool, was blown to earth. The breath of the One condensed in the darkness and water was formed, the moondrop became a drop of dew and the Hum went on all around it. Within the drop of dew was a beautiful magical creature, a Silver Moon Cat who could see beyond Time. The dewdrop melted; the Silver Moon Cat shook herself. All she could hear in the darkness was O-o-o-m-m-m, the sound so strong and the pull of it at her heart so powerful she knew that it must be her real name. Om. Being accidentally born into this worldly dimension she still had the power to appear and disappear at will. She wondered why on earth she was – on earth. It was difficult for her to slot her mind into the restrictions of time and space and gravity and still maintain her awareness of who she really was. She was the Mother of all Cats, she was the mother Goddess Isis, Bastet, Durga, Freya: she was before and beyond time. She was the Pharaoh's daughter and the Buddha's plaything; she was the eye of the moon who shone a light on the path of the lonely at night; she was the guardian of the temples of the ancient lands of the East where humans learnt to be silent and listen to the sound of the heartbeat in the Cosmos, from where she had come, from where they had come, from where all things had come ... only now she was sitting on a patch of warm sunny grass wondering where she had landed this time.

In front of her was a brown square building made of timber from old trees felled half a century ago. The smell of the rainforest pleased her and she walked through the grass to the steps of the building. The door was ajar, and there was a faint scratching sound coming from within. Following it she came to see a small fair skinned boy, alone in the room, studiously drawing a picture.

within the drop of dew was ··· a silver-moon cat

She sat and watched. Then her gaze shifted to the middle distance beyond the Boy so that he was no longer in focus, but she could more clearly perceive now the color of his aura. It was a clear, light gold, the color of the sky washed by dawn on an Australian autumn day. Good, she thought, at least with that color around him he will like me, and I think I might like someone to like me while I am marooned here on earth.

She looked closer. Something had caught her eye in the aura's shadow closer to the Boy's body. Everything about her softened in an air of sadness. Ah, she thought, so that is why I have come here, and at that moment the Boy looked up from his drawing and saw her.

"Oh", he whispered, eyes wide, "what a beautiful cat", and Om shimmered like a moonbeam, looking at him through her azure blue eyes. "Where have you come from?"

"The moon," she prrrped, but he couldn't hear her yet. The Boy put down his pencil and slid off his seat to land on his knees before her (and quite right too, she thought), extending his hand to stroke her head.

"I've never seen a cat like you before," he said softly. "No one on the mountain has one like you. I wonder if I should take you home with me? Ralph Cupboard wouldn't mind a friend."

The Boy stood up and walked to his desk, put away his pencils and folded his drawing paper carefully into his small case, put his chair neatly under the desk, and walked across the classroom calling to the Cat who willingly followed, and he closed the door behind them. He snicked the wooden latch pin so that the winds that blew up from the ferny gullies wouldn't wreck the door, or, blowing and swinging, frighten the bush creatures that came out at night to forage for apple-cores and sandwich crumbs left from lunch. The teacher went to great lengths to explain to the children the philosophical and ecological difference between organic and inorganic rubbish. The latter was scrupulously cleared away and put in rubbish bins: the former, if it was edible and organic, was carefully spread around the perimeter of the schoolhouse garden for possums and pademelons, scrub turkeys, and noisy pittas. Only bones from cooked chicken were excluded, for these were brittle and could splinter and get caught in an animal's throat.

Om followed the Boy down the quiet road until he turned left along a graded bush track and the canopy of whispering gums closed over their heads, filtering the sunlight and acting as a buffer against the afternoon breeze that sprang from the misty gullies hundreds of feet below. The scent of the eucalyptus and the heady perfume of the pittasporam made the Cat's head light – this part of the earth was an okay place to be. The Boy seemed happy to walk at her pace while she paused now and then to listen in the silent bush for the sounds of life. When they reached a house, almost eclipsed by the great trees that stood like prayers around it, the Boy called: "C'mon Cat, this is where we live," and he ran ahead to tell his mother to welcome his new friend.

The Boy's mother was a plump woman of middle age. She had married late in life and she and her husband had waited a long time before she was blessed with Patrick. From his birth he had been a quiet, somewhat introspective child, preferring the company of animals and insects to that of his peers. It wasn't that he didn't like friends it was just that he couldn't keep up with their interests, so many of which centered round physical activities or sports. Whenever he did feel enthusiastic enough to play in the school sports he tired so easily. Gradually his tiredness slipped into a kind of daydreaming and 'Reen and her husband were concerned enough about it to mention it to their local doctor. The Boy had undergone many tests both in hospital and at the local surgery and when the doctor told 'Reen and Dave the prognosis they were practical enough to take his advice to move to clearer air but too stunned to ever mention the diagnosis he gravely gave them. They swore between them they would not tell their son but would allow him whatever he wished in life, Lord knows he wanted little enough it seemed. His greatest love was Ralph Cupboard, the marmalade cat he had rescued from a plastic bag washed up on the beach with six kittens all drowned and tiny Ralph barely alive. He carried the little, pathetic scrap home and between 'Reen, hot water bottles, eye droppers of warm milk, and Pluravit the tiny mite survived to become a most handsome animal with green gold-flecked eyes and a fluffy tail that waved like a banner in a permanent question mark. He was a beautiful natured creature and quite devoted to the Boy. His favorite sleeping place when the Boy was away at school was the jam cupboard ... so he became, for the Boy, Ralph Cupboard. When the family had found the mountains of Springbrook, Ralph Cupboard had happily moved with them and obviously loved the small bush cottage in the trees with its old fashioned verandah and tin roof that sang when the rain fell.

"Mum," called the Boy excitedly, "Mum c'mon see this beautiful cat – she just walked into school and I told her to come home with me and she did. No one owns her Mum, I'm sure. We can keep her can't we?"

'Reen blinked at the beautiful silvery pale animal now

picking her way knowingly and daintily up the wooden steps. She had never seen such a lovely cat before. Her first thought was that Ralph might be a little put out, and, almost as immediately, that such a cat would be bound to have a home and an owner somewhere – and almost simultaneously the third thing that happened to her mind was a kind of blank acceptance. She wasn't to know that the Cat had perceived her doubts and had sent a rapid "all is well" signal across the beam of light that went from the Cat's azure blue eyes to 'Reen's light gray gaze.

"Well," said 'Reen, slightly bemused, "she looks like she's made herself at home, you'd better introduce her to Ralph Cupboard and see how they get on, it's his home after all."

The Boy went to get the big marmalade cat from the warm airy jam cupboard and bundling him up in his arms he told Ralph Cupboard that he had a friend, a really beautiful friend, that he, the Boy, just knew Ralph would like. Ralph didn't know about that but ... and there she was. Om was by now sitting in the center of the verandah and she seemed to be surrounded by a shimmering light like the glowworms and the fireflies on the rainforest walks that Ralph and the Boy sometimes went on at dusk. Ralph's immediate reaction was to stiffen. The Boy put him down and Ralph stared at this moon-like creature. Something in his cat brain cleared, as if a faculty of perception from another dimension had awakened, and he quite distinctly perceived this cat creature say to him without any sound whatever: I am Om, I am the Cosmic Sound; I am not of your kind and though I am like you I am not of your race or reality. Be at peace gentle cat, we both love your Boy and he needs us for his journey.

The Boy and his mother watched in surprise as Ralph seemed to blink and crouch low with his head on his chin: "as if he was paying his respects," laughed 'Reen. "Well," she added, "they don't mind each other so she can stay until someone claims her."

At that a look of pain shot across the Boy's face and he said: "Oh, Mum, I know she doesn't belong to anyone, please don't advertise too hard, I really want her and I know she wants to be here with us too. Please?"

'Reen thought for a moment and then said: "Okay, I'll just let Merv know in the store, if anyone has really lost her he'll be the first person they'd ask – and we'll leave it at that, eh?"

"Oh," breathed the Boy, "thanks Mum. What'll I call her?"

Om took her gaze from Ralph Cupboard (a most handsome cat she thought kittenishly, if I was an Ordinary Cat I'd quite fancy him ...) and sighed and looked directly at the Boy and then 'Reen. She was not going to be called anything except what she was but here in daylight consciousness it was not the time for her to reveal to the Boy her real name. A shaft of afternoon sunlight caught her eyes and she deflected the light in a prism back to the eyes of the two humans watching her, causing them to forget what they had been thinking.

"Better show her the food place," said 'Reen. "Get out one of those blue saucers from the top cupboard for her food and she and Ralph can share the same water bowl."

Om knew she would have to make a pretense of eating ordinary food so as not to arouse suspicion – but in truth she was like the legendary chakor bird who feeds on moonbeams and she didn't need food, just crystal water from the rain now and then. On this mountain there were no pipes carrying water and the people who lived there either collected the water in huge tanks on stilts at the side of their houses or else connected a tap to one of the many springs of clear water that warrened the whole mountain, thus giving it the name of Springbrook. Either water source suited Om perfectly.

Later, when Dave drove in and parked his old ute, clutching the mail and the milk, he too was enchanted with the new cat and when Om blinked her flawless eyes in his direction any questions of her origin and ownership fled his mind too.

CHAPTER FOUR

THE BEGINNING...

Night falls early in the tropics and subtropics – like a velvet curtain, dark and dense. One moment the sky is ablaze with purples and mauves, flame and blood-orange, azure and gold, the clouds shifting and changing, and then, almost as you watch, the light simply drains away beyond the horizon and night has begun.

It is then the bush becomes alive. Australian rainforest dwellers are diurnal or nocturnal apart from the wealth of bird life in that region, and it is the patient watcher who is now rewarded by entree into this magical world of the forest creatures of the night. The ringing calls of the currawongs and the shrill whistle of the kites of the daytime give way to the haunting, muted calls of the mopoke, the boobook or the barking owls from their velvety cover. The wide-eyed possums in their dense silver-gray fur are lit by the moon and, sadly, too often dazzled by headlights too fast to escape from. Diminutive sugar gliders spread their soft furry membrane, winged from fingers to toes, and glide silently from fig tree to eucalypt in search of food; the bandicoot and doe-eyed pademelons forage through the leaves for roots and fallen fruit. The wind dies down and the air is still, so still, until night gives way to dawn, the Australian dawn ... the quietest pageant on earth.

The Boy, under some duress from Dave, had completed his homework. It wasn't that he didn't want to do it, it was just that he was so enraptured with his new friend he simply couldn't take his eyes off her – though all she did was sit.

"C'mon Ralph," he said at last, "let's show Cat our bed, she can sleep on the other side." Ralph Cupboard always sprawled along the left side of the Boy and nothing would shake either of them until morning.

Om of course would not sleep, it was at night that her work was done. The darkness in the Boy's aura, between the golden color and the skin, had told her what she needed to know. She thought she would wait for a night or two until she felt the Boy was ready to see before she would begin. Her timing had to be right.

She curled up on the end of the bed and watched and waited until the Boy and his cat had drifted off to sleep.

Then she sat up. She began to hum, to purr the ceaseless purring that only cats can do; the ceaseless rhythm like the cyclic breathing and playing of the didgeridoo, like the ancient chanting of the Lamas of Tibet – exactly like the eternal vibration that is sacred beyond all sacred sounds she began to purr. Very softly the silence around the sound grew larger, denser, and her purr and the sound of the Humming merged together to become A-A-A-O-O-O-M-M-M. She was back in her other world.

Quite suddenly the Boy sat upright from his sleep. He blinked, letting his eyes grow accustomed to the pale moonlight pouring in through the bedroom window. Bush people never close their curtains, preferring to know they are part of the night and not separate like city folk thought of themselves. He saw the Cat was sitting upright also, on the end of his bed. She sat very still and looked and looked into the Boy's eyes. The Boy blinked again. The silence around him was enormous. Then he heard a sound, he almost felt a sound coming out of the silence. At first he thought it came from the Cat, and he keened his ears to focus in her direction: it wasn't from her but it seemed to come through her. The sound became louder, but not closer, and the world around him, all the sounds he was accustomed to in the night, stood still. No wind stirred, no leaf ruffled, no owl called, no bandicoot rustled: there was a kind of stillness, a holiness like a mystery. Mesmerized, transfixed, the Boy, who couldn't have moved or called out even had he wanted to, realized he could distinguish three distinct yet perfectly blended sounds like an A-A-O-O-M-M, and the most riveting of the sounds was the silence that carried on after the M-M-M was gone. In that silence louder than sound the Boy saw the whole world before time and before shape. Everything that ever was, everything that was as he knew, and everything that was to come, the Boy saw in one lightning flash in his mind's eye, in that dark space behind the eyebrows in the center of his forehead. He knew he would never, ever be able to use words to tell anyone – and as always when a mystery is too overpowering all one can do is obey.

The Humming stopped. The Silver Moon Cat sat quite still, still looking at the Boy. The Boy knew.

"Om," said the Silver Moon Cat, "is my name. I carry that sound from the other worlds to the hearts of those who can hear without ears, and to those whose Dreamdoors are open. I am the guide, I am …"

And she stopped.

The Boy realized he was hearing her without words – he framed a question with thoughts in his mind,

"Show me who you are, show me who you are beautiful Cat, and tell me why you have come to me."

Om's thoughts flew back to the Boy:

"I will show you who I am, but I cannot tell you why I have come to you, that you will know for yourself, soon, soon. You must close your eyes and listen to my voice as your own inner voice and be guided by what I say and do just as I guide you to do. I will take you on a journey and you will see …"

CHAPTER FIVE

THE FIRST JOURNEY...

The Boy nodded in wonderment and agreement. Om settled herself down on her paws, tucking her two front ones under her pale chest and closing her eyes to a slit, looking for all the world like a little Cat Buddha.

"Now," came the words across to the Boy, "sit cross-legged and close your eyes. Pull that coverlet over your shoulder and wrap it round you – don't wake Ralph Cupboard – put your hands on your knees. Good. Keep your spine straight all the time. In fact," paused Om, thinking, "you can tuck your pillow under your bottom because that helps the spine to stay straight and your legs fall crossed more easily. Now just touch together your thumb and the first finger on each hand – that keeps the Cosmic energy flowing."

Om paused for the Boy to do all the adjusting that was necessary and when he was still she began to breathe into her throat to create her own purring sound. Her thoughts began to formulate again and she sent them to the Boy who by now was as motionless as a statue.

"Take your mind deep, deep inside" said a voice, and the Boy did not know whether it was from Om or his own inner voice – he simply obeyed. "Listen to your breath, begin to see your breath; when you breathe in visualize your breath starting at the base of your spine and moving up up up along the spine to the very top of your head, and then when you breathe out follow the breath from the top of your head as it flows all the way down to the base of your spine and comes to rest. Don't change the breath's rhythm" said the voice, "just let the awareness in your mind flow with it – up and down your spinal column with your in breath and your out breath." Effortless.

The Boy's awareness went deeper and deeper in to the rhythm of his own breathing, so deep was he that even the voice grew faint. He began to hear an inner sound, the sound of his own breath. When he breathed in the sound was like a gentle hiss, "so-o-o," and when he breathed out the sound was a hum, "hu-u-m-m." He could hear nothing but the sound of his breath and see nothing but the infinite space inside him.

The voice, very faint and clear like a star, said: "Now stop the awareness of your breath and search for the space around your heart. Not the heart that belongs to your body," continued the cool, clear voice, "but the space that surrounds the heart. See that the space has no limits, no boundaries, it goes on and on, to the north and to the south, to the East and to the West, forever and ever, this space fills eternity."

With his eyes closed the Boy could see within himself, as if with an inner eye, an eye of light. The space indeed went on forever.

"Go to the center of that space," he heard, "go deep, deep into the center of that space and see before you a glorious flower. The flower is large, it has large pinky-mauve petals, there are twelve of them, go up close to it and count them. It sits on a thick, dark green stem, which rises out of a lake of deepest blue water. The center of this flower is quite solid, like the surface of the moon, palest lime green with dark craters."

The Boy was lost in its beauty. Never had he seen a water lily like it and as soon as he had thought of the name he heard his guiding voice say: "No, I am not a water lily, I am a lotus and you can step inside me and see what secrets I hold."

The Boy stepped lightly on to the crater center of the lotus and as he did so the petals fell open to reveal another lake, a lake of crystal blue light within the center of the lotus and there was a boat, a small boat, a sailboat whose mast was a bulrush and whose sail was a thousand flower petals. He knew he had to step into the boat and sail across to the tiny island he could see in the center of this lake.

A breath hummed, the breeze caught the sail, and they were away. Closer and closer he came to the island, and he stared and stared at the tree in the center of it: the tree was perfect. It had large leaves of all the greens that leaves could ever be and white flowers like stars sprinkled among them. Underneath the tree, sitting exactly as Om had told him to sit (a lifetime ago it seemed) the Boy saw a man with a fawn sitting at his left side, and a leopard sitting at his right. Some beautiful birds were in front of them. They were all sitting in perfect harmony and the light surrounding them was palest gold.

"Patrick," said a voice "I am the Kalpa-taru, the wish fulfilling tree. No one usually finds me from your world because I am hidden in the heart space. It is because of Om that you have found me, she has taken you back through your

... and whose sail was a thousand flower petals.

own Dreamdoors to the place your soul lives eternally."

"Ooh," breathed Patrick, and paused. Then he said impulsively,

"Can I see my soul? Is it real? Will I remember all this when I wake up in the morning? Can you show me my soul?"

The pale gold light glistened on the leaves of the Kalpa-taru, the wish fulfilling tree, and it shimmered as if with laughter:

"Small boy, you will see your soul sooner than most, and clearer than most, but you have more journeys to go on with Om first. You must understand All Things so that when the body you think you know as Patrick dies then your soul can come to its Imperishable Home. You see, only half understanding or half believing leads to only half seeing, and with only half seeing you will never really see your soul," sighed the Kalpa-taru. "This means that your journey has to keep on including a body on the plane you know as earth. Mind you," concluded the Tree, "you must be able to see an awful lot already to have brought Om to you, she hasn't been earthbound for a very long time ..."

The Boy bowed his head and said quietly to the Kalpa-taru,

"Well actually I don't think I do know very much because I didn't call Om to me, she was just there when I looked up."

The Tree rustled its leaves:

"Your soul called her only you couldn't hear it ..." and the voice whispered like leaves so that the Boy wasn't quite certain if he heard it or imagined that he had heard it. The leaves rustled again and this time the voice seemed to come from the beautiful radiant man sitting so still under the Kalpa-taru: "Sometimes we don't know that we know ..." and faded away with the slight breeze that sprang up from the South.

The Boy heard another, more distant voice, calling him to leave the lake and the Kalpa-taru and the holy man and the radiant golden peace and to step back into the boat and sail to the edge of the crystal lake. To return to the lotus at the heart and to move into the rhythm of his own breath again, the ceaseless rhythm that continued with the heartbeat of the Cosmos. Dimly the Boy heard a faint chant: "Wolves and lambs will live together in peace and leopards will lie down with young goats." He shook his head, it seemed vaguely familiar but he couldn't say where he had heard it before and as he was racking his brain he heard with absolute clarity the voice of the Kalpa-taru resonating from deep inside him even though he could no longer see the Tree: "You must go with Om beyond Time, see All Things as One and return to know the Dreaming of your own land. Then your journey is over."

The Boy shivered and realized where he was, sitting up in bed wrapped in a coverlet, Ralph Cupboard sound asleep beside him, and Om his beautiful Silver Moon Cat at the end of his bed still watching him. She sent her thoughts to him to

The wish-fulfilling tree ∴ Kalpa taru

tell him to lie down, to sleep, this night he would not dream because he had visited the world where dreams come from. In the morning he would go to school as normal and tell no one where he had been and tomorrow night Om would take him on his second journey.

CHAPTER SIX

KNOWING...

There was a knock on the door and 'Reen stepped into the room calling: "Patrick, time to get up. Dad has left early this morning so go and shower while I get breakfast."

Ralph opened his golden-green eyes and stretched, touching the Boy's cheek with one pink padded paw, then he slid off the bed and followed 'Reen to get his own breakfast. Om sat quietly on the coverlet. The Boy awoke, looked at the trellis of gum leaves at the window and wondered if what he had experienced was all a dream.

"No," beamed the voice from the Cat, "you did not dream it, it was real and now you know that my name is Om call me and I will nod my head and prrrp three times to convince you that where we go is not a dream, and nor am I."

Very steadily the Boy looked at the silvery Cat and tentatively, finding his voice, said, with an early morning huskiness: "Om? Are you Om? Is that your name?"

Om nodded her head and prrrped three times. She opened her eyes wide, looked across into his and said through his thoughts: "In daytime consciousness you will not be able to hear me clearly. Once you are out and about I will seem as any other cat to anyone else, only you will know the difference but you will only be able to hear me and speak with me on the doorway of sleep each night. Stay keen young friend, keep on with your school work and ordinary life. I'll see you tonight."

The Boy reached out and stroked her head, got out of bed, grabbed his shorts and T-shirt and made his way quickly to the shower. He could hear his mother flicking the toaster and switching on the kettle and picking the oranges out of the hanging basket that held the fruit. All these sounds were as sharp as if he was hearing them for the first time. He turned on the shower and the rushing water enveloped him. Ten minutes later he was sitting at the solid scrubbed pine kitchen table eating his breakfast while his mother packed his lunch, which today consisted of a curried egg sandwich, a tomato, a couple of juicy tamarillos from the vine by the water tank, a muesli bar and a crisp apple.

The whole mountain range that made up Springbrook had rich volcanic soil from which grew in abundance fruits such as tamarillos and avocados. On the plains below between the southern tip of the ranges around Murwillumbah and Tumbulgum all the way to Blue Knob and Lillian Rock were plantations of sugarcane and bananas. It was an area of great fertility and great beauty and the family often spent one of the weekend days exploring the patchwork plains or the magnificent coastlines.

The Boy especially loved that area of coastal dunes between Kingscliff and Hastings Point, miles and miles of it, the amaranthine coastline, the whispering glades of casuarinas carpeted with fleshy pink flowering pigface and the white sand, soft and dry and fine, that squeaked as he walked on it. Here were a hundred different birds – rainbow-birds, flowerpeckers, silvereyes, honeyeaters, dollar birds – and in the bush back from the sea spoonbills and pelicans on the inner lakes. They were all quite different to the shy rainforest birds the Boy was familiar with on the high escarpments. From the coast he especially liked looking at Mt. Warning, its aspect so different from the lion's pose he was used to seeing from the Springbrook lookouts.

When the wind blew from the west, embracing the mountain's thoughts, it seemed to carry to the Boy a whispered reminder not to forget how to tread lightly on this earth, not to forget that he was to walk as gracious guest – and the Boy's heart ached. He knew the song from the soul of this timeless soil was unheeded by most of the white people who were too busy to hear the earth's whisper above the buzz of chainsaws, thunder of bulldozers, and dreams of dollars in ever increasing bank balances.

He walked slowly to the schoolhouse, his head oddly still after the night's experiences. At a deep corner of his being the Boy knew that nothing was strange, that in fact he had always known such experiences could happen – almost as if what had happened was a replay of something in his memory long forgotten. He knew no one would claim Om, knew she was his and his only, and that there was a special reason for her being there. Often he worried about his tiredness and the way he bruised so easily at even the slightest knock, and he worried even more because he didn't want to worry his parents. He had a vague idea all the tests he had had when they were living in Adelaide were part of the reason why the family had moved to Springbrook. But when he asked that kind of question his mother was never very enthusiastic about giving a straight answer so he gave up asking. He was pretty sure his tiredness worried them.

Back in the house Om cleaned herself and walked to one of the verandahs to settle herself in a patch of dappled sunlight and sleep for the day. Just as she was settling down she remembered with a mild reproof at her negligence that she had forgotten to explain to the Boy that when one enters into one's inner world as deeply as he had the result is a tremendous surge of energy which comes up from the inner depths to spill over into waking activities. That in itself didn't matter at all, in fact a good burst of energy to counteract the tiredness from his illness would do no harm whatever, but what was important and what Om had forgotten to explain to him was how to contain it, not to dissipate it, to keep it within himself and not lose it and end up even more tired than before. She thought seriously about walking to the school-house, but visions of being patted by dozens of hands and knowing it was unlikely she could get these thoughts through to Patrick without the silence necessary to explain what she meant, stopped her.

She remembered today was sports afternoon and once again the Boy would be on his own so perhaps the energy would simply transfer itself to some particularly expressive drawing. There was the hint of a prickly feeling in the center of her forehead, but when she tried to focus on it to give it meaning, and dialogue, it slipped away. Om herself was tired from the night's journey, she hadn't yet comfortably adjusted to being back in a dimension of dual consciousness.

To the Boy everything this morning seemed brilliant. All that he could see had a crystal clarity about it that he had not noticed before. It was as if his seeing had been cleansed. The titian hair of the little girl in the front row glistened with a trillion lights that altogether made up the titian but, in his reality, were actually blends of every other color. The leaves outside were not green anymore either, they were shades and tones and hints and blends of so many colors that then made up a vision of greens.

Something was bubbling up inside him and he wanted to sing and even dance with joy. Instead he smiled to himself as if he held a great secret, precious and rare. Somewhere far away, he wasn't sure whether it was inside him or outside him, he could hear a great Hum, and he knew it was the sound, the eternal sound, of the name of his Silver Moon Cat. Then he remembered the Kalpa-taru, the wish fulfilling tree that lives in the heart, and he knew the sound Om came from inside, from the inner planes.

The morning passed quickly. The teacher spent much of the morning periods with a new girl about the same grade as the Boy. She had come from another State and the teacher was poring over the different textbooks to prepare some framework for him to help her. He was too busy to notice the high flush of color on Patrick's cheeks, the clear light in his eye and the animation around his lips.

At 12.40 the school monitor rang the bell. Lunchtime, then sports. It was tricky trying to play any kind of organized sports with such an assortment of sizes, shapes, and ages of children, so the teacher usually let the children form natural groups or couples and choose any physical activity they liked. He himself took turns at being with each group or couple for fifteen minutes or so and sharing in whatever they planned to do. There was a series of metal gymnastic frames in the garden and also two swings. The younger children who chose swings had to think of a number they would like to do and do just that many, then they had to move on to something else. It was a gentle and encouraging way of teaching self-discipline and trust. The teacher never checked the number of swings, but each child intuitively knew the importance of carrying out his or her own task knowing the responsibility they held was entirely their own. The teacher was the kind of person who naturally trusted his children and it was unthinkable to the children to betray that trust, no matter how they behaved at home.

The teacher felt a special bond with Patrick. His parents were simple and uncomplicated and had calmly and matter-of-factly come to tell him that Patrick had leukemia but was to continue school as normally as possible. His tiredness and physical fragility excluded him from sports but if he wanted to fill in the afternoon at school by drawing or going for short walks in the National Park that bounded the school then he was to be encouraged to do so. They were not telling Patrick that his tiredness was caused by a terminal illness. No one, argued Dave sagely, can really predict a life or a death and to live having been told you are dying was not a sensible way for a child to make the most of living. As he said to the teacher, life was only one breath long, and if you didn't make the next one you were a goner – might as well get on and live. "You can forget dying," he muttered as an afterthought, "it remembers itself."

The teacher thought this was probably the best way for the moment. Perhaps Patrick would not suffer pain, a lot of people who had leukemia didn't suffer pain particularly – but some do. What then?

"We'll jump that hurdle when we come to it," answered 'Reen. And there they left it.

Lunch over, the bell rang again and the children began to organize themselves for the afternoon. Patrick was still feeling full of a strange excitement, he felt like jumping up and down and one of the younger girls told him he looked like Alice's Cheshire Cat and Patrick grinned even more. Not the Cheshire Cat he thought, a Silver Moon Cat.

He decided for the afternoon that he would go for a walk to the top of Purlingbrook Falls and look out across the escarpment to the misty blue trees on the lower foothills that seemed to reach to the sea sparkling in the distance many miles away. It only seemed that the forests met the sea. In actual fact, right on the edge of the shore, so it seemed from the mountain, were a dozen or more bright, white concrete fingers of holiday apartments which were part of the Gold Coast landscape at Surfers Paradise. They punctuated the view and, from up here, didn't fit at all comfortably into the dazzling panorama.

Sitting there, sometimes gazing into the far distance, sometimes focusing on a line of ants attempting to maneuver a tiny ball of honey resin from one of the myriad plants surrounding him, the Boy was still enough to hear the radiant man underneath the Kalpa-taru as his inner voice whispered: "Sometimes we don't know that we know ..."

With an exultant whoop the Boy sprang up and raced along the winding pressed earth path with mossy rocks and roots straggling from one side to the other, treacherously hidden by the fallen leaves and ferns. The wind caught his face and the Boy gave a cry of happiness ... at that instant Om sprang awake, she knew what the prickly sensation was.

Suddenly the Boy's heel caught a slippery root, his foot twisted in pain and he fell clumsily and heavily to the ground, catching his forehead on a rock in the high earth to his left.

Om saw it happen in her mind's eye. Forcing herself to

dematerialize she appeared on the forest track near the Boy. He was concussed. She thought for a moment – how could she mobilize people to find the Boy without them being sidetracked by her seemingly unworldly and magical antics? Ralph Cupboard, she thought, if she could convey the accident to him he could behave accordingly and 'Reen would know something must be the matter with the Boy as the pair of them were so close.

Within seconds Om was padding her way to the jam cupboard to make contact with the sleeping Ralph. He heard her come in and looked down from his top shelf.

"The Boy has been hurt," Om beamed up to Ralph. "I am too unusual to make 'Reen understand it is for the Boy that I am attracting her attention, you will have to do it. She knows how close you are to him and unusual behavior from you will alert her. I will send pictures to her mind of what has happened and where she can find her child. Come with me quickly, he is on the upper path that runs under Purlingbrook waterfall."

Ralph was immediately on the floor beside her. He nodded and said silently through his thoughts to Om: "We'll find 'Reen doing her embroidery – this her day for it."

'Reen looked up and smiled at the sight of the two cats

padding across the polished wooden floor but when Ralph wound round her legs and made little growls and ran to the door and then returned and did the same thing again she stopped smiling and put down her embroidery intent on trying to understand what he was trying to tell her.

Om sat very still and framed the scene where Patrick had fallen as a picture in her mind. She concentrated with all her might on the space behind 'Reen's eyebrows. She knew she could focus the thoughts and the picture in there, it was just a question of receptivity. 'Reen was concentrating too hard.

'Reen knelt on the floor and said: "Ralph I know you are trying to tell me something but I don't know what, or how I can hear." And Om told Ralph to sit very still for 'Reen to stroke him and that would calm her and would act as a space for Om to project her pictures.

Ralph did as he was told and 'Reen ran her hand over his head. Almost at once her mind cleared and in her mind's eye she could see Patrick lying hurt on the forest track. Her hand flew to her face, she stood up, and when Om ran to the door she followed automatically. The thoughts in her head stopped and she trusted this strange cat implicitly.

There was a short cut to that particular path from the end

of their road where the few house block subdivisions ended at the forest edge. Om and 'Reen ran swiftly to reach Patrick who by now was sitting up feeling very faint and whose ankle was swelling with pain. 'Reen sat down beside him.

"Oh Patrick, it was Ralph and the new cat who told me where you were, how on earth did they know I wonder? But anyway here we are, do you feel able to hop the short track home if I support you?"

"Yes, I'll try," said Patrick, "and her name is Om, Mum, and she knows everything and ah-h-h-h," he cried out in pain as 'Reen helped him balance on his one good foot.

The ten-minute walk took over half an hour, tears at times bursting from the Boy's eyes as the uneven path made even leaning on his mother difficult. 'Reen got him into bed and then telephoned the doctor who ran the center he called Raphael, after the Archangel of Healing, not far from them.

He was a most unusual doctor. As a young man he believed he could not heal the body without healing the spirit as well, and after graduating from medicine had spent the next few years studying to be a priest. He had bought many hundreds of acres on Springbrook with the vision of a Healing Center and quite by chance had discovered a small grove of twelve massive conifers, rare in that part of the world, on the land. Immediately he knew that here he would create the Tree Chapel. The altar had been made from huge logs felled long ago, and the cross was two perfectly natural arms from a fallen mountain gum, white and highly polished. Circles were sawn from old fallen timber to set as seats amidst the stand of conifers, the Twelve Apostles as they came to be known. 'Reen and Dave had been over almost a year ago now, to the Easter Vigil when they had first come to the mountain, but they were not, as a rule, churchgoers. The Boy sometimes went for a walk that way and sat under the huge pines listening to the wind that he said to himself sounded like the breath of God.

The shock was beginning to tell on the Boy – he was very pale and his head was bruised where he had fallen. The doctor gave him a sedative and strapped up his ankle and suggested as much rest as possible. And definitely no walking for three days. After that if he felt up to it he could get out of bed. The sedative was a strong one and the Boy was sound asleep when the old ute rumbled into the drive and Dave climbed out, thankful to be home.

In the kitchen he found 'Reen making a pot of tea.

"Sit down," she said quietly. "Patrick is in bed, he had a

fall and Doctor Jefferson gave him a sedative. He's okay, just shaken with a very bruised ankle. Got to rest for three days. The weird thing was that it was the cats who told me, and the new one ran with me to where Patrick had fallen, just as if she knew. Come to think of it, when we got there Patrick said she was called, um, Um or Om or something and that she knew everything ..."

Dave took the cup of tea 'Reen had poured for him. He looked at Om sitting upright in the center of the floor, looking directly at him.

"I think he may be right. There is something different about her, the way she looks at me now makes me think she can see straight through me to somewhere I don't even know about. She's not your average mog, 'Reen, y'know."

Dave thoughtfully stroked his chin. He wasn't one for a romantic view of life but somehow since the Boy's illness he had become aware of another dimension to his nature and he found himself saying: "I wonder if she's come here for a purpose, y'know, something to do with Pat's illness."

'Reen just nodded; she had the same odd feeling. It was good how close this had brought the pair of them, good to know that the kind of thoughts that were never normally spoken were in fact shared. As if on cue Om rose and turned to walk to the Boy's room to join him and Ralph. Tonight she would watch carefully, there would be no journey until the sedatives were right out of his system.

CHAPTER SEVEN

THE DREAMING...

It had been a few days since the Boy had woken naturally from his sleep to sit with Om on another journey. The sedatives and potions he had been given by the doctor made his sleep heavy and Om knew it was important for the Boy's system to clear itself before her work could begin again.

The night continued like any other: Om sitting like a silvery white statue on the end of the Boy's bed, Ralph stretched out on the Boy's left side, the Boy sleeping – but now not so heavily. Om could feel that his breathing had changed, it was lighter, he was lighter, and then the Boy stirred.

As his head moved from side to side he frowned and through his sleep he moaned: "Om, Om-m-m."

Within minutes he sat up slowly, rubbing his eyes, blinking, unsure.

"Oh, Om," his thoughts whispered, "I feel I've been away such a long time – I've been waiting to talk to you again."

Om lowered her eyelids and sent back to him: "I have been waiting for you too. Tonight will be very important if you feel up to it, do you? Good, because I am not taking you back in time, only in space. You know," she went on, "that some people, the People who belong, have always understood that the soil upon which they were born actually carries their soul. When the land dies the soul of its people dies too. Then they become treacherous, ruthless, destructive and because they are not aware of what has died within them they intuitively seek to destroy the land, the soul of other people. This earth," sighed Om, "is dying slowly, some of its people are killing it by degrees. They do not mean the killing to happen, they do not mean to say goodbye but whole animal tribes are dying, whole rivers and seas and forests – it will not be long," said Om, "before there is nothing left."

The Boy's eyes filled with tears, he knew it: had read in his schoolbooks of how white men had murdered and nearly wiped out the Red Indian. The Red Indian who knew the rhythm of the earth's song humming through his moccasin'd soles, who was elder brother to the animals and trees. He knew he was like the Little Mouse who jumped and caught a glimpse of the Sacred Mountains. His teacher, who loved the earth, shared his love with the children, and read them stories from many lands. The Boy thought over to Om: "Om did you know the Mouse who Jumped? I feel like that mouse. I don't know if I would be brave enough or big enough to let Buffalo or Gray Wolf have my eyes because they were Great Beings but I know that I am different and the sight of the Sacred Mountains burns in my heart and I must reach them myself."

Om smiled to herself. Certainly she knew Jumping Mouse who became Eagle; certainly she knew the rhythm the Red Indians call the Give Away Dance, for all beings had to learn their Give Away before they could see or hear Love. She knew All Things. She knew the Red Indian Medicine Wheel and she knew too that it was almost too late for the Red Indian to move to that rhythm again. Unless she was called to earth by many more children whose Dreamdoors were open so that they could learn their place in the Universe, could learn their own Give Away Dance, could listen to their own Myth.

"There is no one of any of the animals in the world that can do without the next," said Om. "Each whole tribe of animals is a Medicine Wheel in that it is One Mind. Parts of these tribes must Give Away in order that they all might grow. The animal tribes all know this. It is only people who must learn it. The Red Indians know that white men have never understood the Medicine Gift from the Earth their Mother. We have to ask Who Am I? What is my Medicine? In what way do I Perceive? Each person is born with a different animal medicine from which they receive their own Medicine Way – even though we may perceive this differently. For you I became a Cat."

Om paused to see if the Boy truly perceived the Wisdom that she was saying in this simple analogy. She remembered what the Kalpa-taru had whispered to him on his first journey: "Sometimes we don't know that we know ..." She wanted to be sure that he knew that he knew.

"In the land of Jumping Mouse," she continued, "the animals are not the same as in your land, or in other lands, but the Law of the Give Away Dance is always the same. For Jumping Mouse learnt that She Wolf was hungry for Buffalo and Buffalo hungers to Give Away to She Wolf. Just as

Jumping Mouse hungered to Give Away his eyes (even though he was terribly, terribly afraid) so that the Great Beings could live. All give in this manner. It is the Way of Understanding. It is a Perfect Circle. Jumping Mouse did not know that by Giving Away his eyes he would become Eagle, carried by the wind to see All Things. It is in the Give Away Dance that we learn of our Perceiving. Each one of us has to Give Away that which is most dear."

"You see," said Om, "this is a Myth, a Way of Perceiving, and we must all find our own Give Away."

Om knew the Boy was very close to his own Give Away Dance and it would be a different Myth, using different words, and it would be his own way of Perceiving. Om was the guide for the Boy to know the greatest Give Away Dance of all. But she held her thoughts.

The Boy was far away. He knew most people were too busy with their lives to worry about answering his questions about his own dream of the Sacred Mountains.

He thought to Om: "Once I said to Gran when she was still alive that I wanted to see God and she laughed at me and said I could only see God if I was dead. That's sort of like the Give Away isn't? Jumping Mouse had to Give Away his eyes, but he didn't know he was going to become Eagle who could see Everything. And Everything is God."

Om sat very still. The point of her being with the Boy was not for her to say yes or no but to help him reveal his own Way of Understanding, which could only come from the depth of his heart where the Seed of Love lies.

Tonight he would find the Myth of the People of the land he loved and knew as Australia. He would hear the Dreaming, because this was the Land that carried the Soul.

"I'm ready," he said, sitting in the cross-legged pose Om had showed him a couple of nights before. He began to breathe into his throat so that it felt as if the breath didn't come from outside himself at all. Up and down the spine it flowed: in – So-o-o, and out – Hum-m-m. Om began her cyclic purring and very soon the Boy heard her voice as if it were his own inner voice, faint and clear like a star, telling him to go again into the space that surrounds the heart; the space that goes on and on to the north and to the south, to the East and to the West, forever and ever. And again the Boy saw within himself as if with an inner eye, an eye of light.

"This time," he heard the voice, "the lotus before you is red, deepest red like blood, like velvet, and all around it is a golden mist, clearest brightest yellow gold. Go up to the petals, the blood red petals, and touch each one in turn. There are twelve of them and they are edged with gold where they merged into the mist. These are the colors of the Dreamtime People, the oldest people in the world, they will show you their Myth, their Way of Perceiving."

The petals of the lotus fell open one by one as the Boy touched them. As he did so he heard an extraordinary sound so old and so powerful that it sounded like the Hum of the earth he had heard on his first night with Om. But it was different; it had a series of waves and pulses that sounded as if it was being forced through something else. It sent shivers up his spine and as he touched the twelfth petal light exploded in the center of the lotus to reveal an old Aboriginal man, as wise as the rocks, playing a didgeridoo. The sound drew him deeper through the center of the lotus, and all around the old man, for as far as his eye could see, the Boy was aware of the shimmering heart of the Desert land, and the haze of heat that almost seemed white in its intensity. He felt the earth burn beneath the soles of his feet, the blistering red earth of the Land of the People. The humming of the didgeridoo now sounded like a breath, as if it was breathing words through its hollow trunk. The Boy strained his ears, surely they were words. If he held his breath he could hear them, why – they were telling him their Myth, they were saying to him the secrets of their Way of Understanding of their place in the Universe.

The voice rippled through the wind of the didgeridoo:

You are a child of the Dreamtime People
Part of the land like the gnarled gum tree.
You are the river softly singing
Chanting your songs on your way to the sea.
Your spirit is the dust devils;
Mirages that dance on the plain.
You are the snow, the wind and the falling rain.
You are part of the rocks and the red desert earth
Red as the blood that flows in your veins.
You are eagle, crow, and snake that glides
Through rainforest that clings to the mountainside.

You awakened here when the earth was new.
There was emu, wombat, and kangaroo.

No other man of different hue!
You are this land and this land is you.

The Boy felt a great heat around his heart; it felt like it would burst, felt like a great tidal wave, filling his whole life. He knew that what he had to Give Away was himself – only when "he" was not there could Love as deep as the Ocean flow through him. It was as if he, the Boy he thought he knew, had been annihilated and he was hollow like the didgeridoo through which blew the Primordial Sound. He almost fainted with the intensity of the experience, but faint and far away like a star, he heard Om whisper to him to look at the lotus, to look closely through the brilliant golden-yellow mist to the center where the petals meet.

The Boy seemed to need a tremendous effort to let the dazzling vision of the Desert go, it drew him into itself until he felt he had no boundaries even to his own body. He blinked and tried to focus on the center of the lotus. There, shimmering like the purest rainbow he had ever seen, around the center of the blood red lotus and shining through the golden mist was ... the most marvelous snake, iridescent and brilliant, a rainbow snake.

The Boy gasped, and blinked again. The snake turned his head to look and speak to the Boy, the words gliding along the sand like a vibration that the Boy drew up from the soil beneath his feet: "I, I am the Rainbow Snake, I am the Myth of my People, from me all things are made known," and there was a slow hiss like a sigh as the Rainbow Snake breathed out the next words: "you must find your own Myth, Patrick, your people have lost their Myth, they have forgotten how to listen to the Sound of Silence, they have stopped hearing the voice of the wind whom the One they call God placed at the end of rainbows." The hissing sound sighed again and the Boy's feet tingled.

"I hold the secrets of this Land and the secrets of the Dreaming. You will know me again, little child, when you meet me under the Kalpa-taru within your heart when you find your own Myth and know All Things are One. Listen to Om-m-m-m-m ..." and the sound went on and on to the furthest point of the Universe.

The Boy felt as if he was falling and falling, spinning and spiraling. Dimly he heard Om's voice whirling around his head.

"Go to the sound of your breathing, hear the sound of your own breath, let everything go, just be still in your own self, breathing in and out, So-hum, along the spine, just think of your breath, let everything else go, slowly, slowly."

Gradually the world stopped its gyrations and the Boy found that he could feel his feet, his legs, and the pins and needles down his right thigh, the touch of the coverlet over his shoulders, could hear his breath and the quiet snore of Ralph Cupboard lost in oblivion. He wriggled his fingers and his toes and very slowly opened his eyes to see Om, in her Cat Buddha pose, motionless on the end of his bed.

The moonlight caught the ghostly white gum outside his window and he felt he knew it like he had never known it before. It was a part of him, like an arm or a leg. He shook his head in wonder at the different way he was perceiving. Om just nodded, and then thought to him: "You must sleep now, all that you have seen and heard are part of the Way of Understanding. Sleep is necessary now for it all to become known inside you. You won't be going to school today so just sleep, sleep as long as you need. I'll be here when you wake."

... part of the rocks and the red desert earth.

CHAPTER EIGHT

AWAKENING...

The Boy slept on. Deep inside him, in the space within the heart where the soul dwells, changes were taking place, a kind of transformation like the caterpillar who sleeps in darkness to emerge as a glorious butterfly. The Greek word for the soul, and their symbol for the soul, was the butterfly – Om knew it, but the Boy had to recall it from his own depths. Symbols, thought Om to herself as she settled down on her four paws on the end of the bed, are the doorway to our soul, and are the signs we need to open our heart to the transcendent Reality. Most people, her thoughts continued, have lost their ability to read symbols, or to stand in awe of the sacred. She guessed she was especially sensitive to feeling like this at the moment because it was so close to Easter and she remembered her time as a temple Cat in the high Himalayas a couple of thousand years ago (just a split second it seemed to her) when darkness filled the whole earth for three hours and the light of a thousand suns went out and the earth trembled and the heavens wept at the murder in the land of Israel of the great, just, Jesus in whom dwelt the Soul of the Universe.

This, she knew, was the Boy's myth. He had to learn of his own myth. The myth that is buried as an archetype in every soul has a penetrating power and carries with it the key to release that which would otherwise be forever buried in the psyche. A myth is so vast, so universal: it draws those whose Dreamdoors are open, whose gate has become the Gateless gate, into the most secret source of their being. It is only then that one is carried to the world invisible, the world intangible; to the place where estranged faces miss the many-splendored thing. The angels indeed keep their ancient places – the Boy had turned the stones and seen their faces. Om had to work on 'Reen and Dave to take the Boy to the Easter Vigil. She thought she might use Dr. Jefferson as her medium, he was a very wise man and understood symbols, and she felt he might even understand the Hint of her being with the Boy.

··the birth of the Child who knew The Way·

It was Thursday. Om quietly left the Boy sleeping and walked to the verandah that faced east. This time she needed to move forward in time as well as back. Here was a corner where she knew she would not be disturbed. She sat on the seagrass matting and looked out across the soft hills on the breadth of the escarpment, green and rolling, covered with thick grass. The other views from the cottage were of rainforest and plunging waterfalls and deep valleys – here was the other side of Springbrook.

"There is a green hill far away, beyond the city wall … where our dear Lord was crucified, who died to save us all …" Funny she should think of that now. The sun was warm and Om began to breathe deep, deep, deep, making the rhythmic purring sound that never ceases. She took herself back to the time when she was under a manger, the Holy Manger; no one saw her there but the sheep and cattle, for she had come as a blessing from the Moon for the Birth of the Child Who Knew The Way.

The Wise Men from the East followed the Star that blazed in the heavens and these were the Men who Knew. No one came from the West. Om felt a tear in her beautiful eyes for she knew the men from the West had never really understood the simple message of the Way. Poets and painters sometimes caught glimpses, but hearts had to learn to open like the Easter Rose, whose head still bowed in shame for the iniquity of mankind. It had bowed its head since those terrible hours of darkness on that Friday when she had bloomed at the foot of the Cross and could not bear the weight of the sorrow of the Man who could say: "Weep not for me, but for yourselves."

So many scenes passed Om's mind screen and when she took her mind to her heart all around her she could hear, like a heavenly chant, the echo of the oldest words that men knew:

"Om, the little space within the heart is as great as this vast Universe. The heavens and earth are there, and the sun and the moon and the stars. Fire and lightning and winds are there; and all that now is and all that is not: for the whole Universe is in Him and He dwells within our heart."

These were the words from the East that the Wise Men sang in their own hearts while they followed the star. When they reached the crib a haunting cry echoed and re-echoed on the roof of the stable: the cry was the peacock who brought her eye of wisdom and message of immortality. She cried for the future where she saw that of the many who would heed the voice and follow the star, only one would walk with Him to Calvary: it was too far.

Later, when the Babe was asleep and the many had gone,

..the Easter rose... had bloomed at the foot of the Cross.

Om came out to drink in the moon's light and she looked up at the peacock who would carry the secret and return to the East where its reproachful cry would echo down centuries.

Om came out of her space and her heart ached. It was a

mixture of pain, for love is not born without pain. She stepped down from the verandah and began to pad along the bush track to Raphael, to the Tree Chapel where the fir trees whispered from the hearts of the Twelve men they symbolized. The grass was long and damp and when she reached the clearing she sat and cleaned herself thoroughly, making certain there were no tiny grass ticks embedded in her pads. She knew Dr. Jefferson or his wife placed fresh flowers on the wooden altar every day and she had arrived in plenty of time so that either of them would be sure to see her.

Taking a quick breath she leapt onto the altar and positioned herself for her meditation. Once more she became as motionless as a statue, as still as a little Cat Buddha, and she breathed, and waited.

Quietly she heard Dr. Jefferson approach. She did not stir. She knew he had seen her and she waited in great peace for him to observe her and when his mind had settled any initial irritation about finding a cat on the altar she would begin to talk to him.

She didn't need much time. Dr. Jefferson was indeed a wise man and he had an inkling, when he had caught a glimpse of Om a couple of days before at the cottage, that she was by no means an ordinary cat. To find her sitting on the altar seemed the harbinger that gave meaning to the premonition that spun like a meteor through his head when he saw the young Patrick last.

"Hullo Cat," he said softly, "do you, uh, want to tell me something?" Om nodded her head. Surprised, Dr. Jefferson sensed immediately that this unusual creature could understand what he said, and in the same span of moment he thought: "But how am I to understand her?"

Immediately he heard, or felt, or saw, the word "pratyahara" stream across his mind screen. Narrowing his eyes he looked at Om, she widened her gaze and beamed across at him: "pratyahara, pratyahara; withdraw your senses, withdraw your senses and hear me with your inner ear, see me with your inner eye."

He knew then that he was in the presence of a mystery – and he obeyed. Sitting on one of the sawn log seats Dr. Jefferson closed his eyes, took a deep breath and then released it, scanning his mind like a laser beam rapidly around the sounds around him. After a moment or two of keeping his mind externalized he withdrew his awareness within to his breath and his mind naturally became still as a consequence of the initial activity. All sound ceased for him, he became clear like a pool, receptive to the inner processes. He began to hear a Hum, a vibration, a sound, a silence. The sound grew louder, but not closer, and the world around him, all the sounds he was accustomed to in the day, stood still. No wind stirred, no leaf ruffled, no currawongs called, no blue-tongued lizard rustled: there was a kind of stillness, a holiness, like a mystery. Very faint and far away like a star the awareness came upon him that he was in the presence of the Cosmic Sound, the Word that was in the Beginning and ever shall be.

Out of the sounds came ripples of smaller sounds, like words, and he knew they came from the Silver Moon Cat sitting on the altar:

"Om," said the Silver Moon Cat, "is my name. I carry that sound from the other worlds to the hearts of those whose Dreamdoors are open. I come as a guide to those who call. The call of the Boy is as old as time, only he doesn't know it. I am the guide for his soul. He has reached the end of his journey, the Journey of journeys is ahead of him now, you must bring him to the Easter Vigil for he has to understand why he called me to him."

Om paused. She could see the man in front of her

tremble. It was so much more difficult to talk to grown-ups because their heads got in the way of their hearts and when at last they heard the whispering murmur of their inner kingdom it often had a very strange effect on them. Dr. Jefferson was not actually thinking any thoughts at all, and Om knew he was receptive and open, aware of what she was beaming over to him. She let him rest in the awareness for a moment and then said: "Tomorrow is the Friday of all Fridays. After that there is the Vigil for those who believe life is eternal, and the Boy will follow the Easter Star that he will see in the night sky. You may see it, you may not, but it will be there, and the Boy will see it – and I will carry his soul on the wind and my work will be done ... for this time and for this Boy. There will always be others of course."

Om stopped. She sat up, stretched, put her paw in the split in the wood grain of the altar and teased a beetle trying to roll a soft newly fallen leaf into its nest. For a divine cat she was very human. She waited, not beaming any more thoughts, until Dr. Jefferson came back from his inner space. Time passed. When he felt there was no more to be heard Dr. Jefferson gently moved his fingers and stretched his legs and slowly opened his eyes.

"Om," he said gently, "the Silver Moon Cat, the Cat from the Moon who lights a path and shows us 'in' sight. This is indeed a mystery. So, you want Patrick to come here for Easter Vigil? His time is so close then?"

Om nodded to affirm for the man that he had not imagined that he had heard.

"I suppose I could tell 'Reen and Dave it was just as a reminder of their arrival here, a kind of annual thanksgiving for finding the mountain. I don't want to cause them any alarm, I haven't told them how close their child is to leaving them y'know."

Om rose, nodded, leapt lightly to the ground and began to walk back across the green meadow leaving Dr. Jefferson to come back to the immediate here and now and work out how to discreetly tell the family he would like them to come to the Vigil. The Boy slept on, deeply and soundly. 'Reen kept looking in but did not disturb him. Ralph Cupboard was with him on the coverlet but the Silver Moon Cat had gone. About mid-morning 'Reen saw Om padding across from the direction of Raphael and the thought occurred to her that it was Easter this weekend. That meant a load of tourists probably, and coach loads of day-trippers for the English

Gardens and the Tulip Farm or the Pottery down along Lyrebird Ridge Road. Well, she reasoned, can't really complain, half a dozen coaches hardly spelt Bondi, Benidorm, or Blackpool. Even so she resented the intrusion. So it seemed, did the mountain. People who fell in love with the place and thought they wanted to move up here were often rejected by the mountain itself, spat out, the local folk said. Funny that, mused 'Reen, she and Dave had had nothing but blessings since they had moved here, they had a lot to be thankful for. Her thoughts trailed like clouds drifting across her mind; thinking of being thankful, when was the last time she had actually said "thank you" to anything for actually finding Springbrook? Hmmm, a year ago in fact. Well, she wasn't one for moping around Easter Friday but the Saturday Vigil with the priest lighting the candle from the bonfire lit to guide the sunrise for the Ascension really appealed to her. She just might go across there on Saturday – better 'phone Dr. Jefferson and ask him what time the service started.

Dr. Jefferson had walked slowly back to his house, crossing the stile and absent-mindedly patting the plump donkeys in the meadow on the way. He took off his shoes as he always did when he entered the inner rooms and sat

and the heavens wept

for in Him dwelt the Soul of the Universe

looking out of the picture window at the scene of great peace in front of him. He was wondering how to tell the Boy's parents to come to the Easter Vigil when the telephone rang. It was 'Reen. The doctor shook his head in wonder and smiled to himself as he answered 'Reen's question. The problem, naturally, had resolved itself.

When Dave returned 'Reen told him she had felt the need to go to the Tree Chapel on Saturday and Dave, fairly non-committal, had replied, "Righto 'Reen, if Pat's up and about we'll go."

Friday dawned, clear and bright. The Boy had slept on and off for hours and hours. When he awoke he seemed to be in another world. Om watched him. She knew he was undergoing inner preparations far beyond anything the conscious mind, attached to "I" awareness, could understand. He wanted to go over to the Tree Chapel, but not during the Mass, he just wanted to be alone.

By mid-afternoon there was an eerie darkness coming up from the valleys to the west of the mountain, as if forces contained within the mountain were being brought together to be released somehow. Clouds, heavy and laden, rumbled and collected together and the wind suddenly sprang up from the gullies, making the clouds jostle and tumble each other in their flight from the force of the wind. Sudden storms often happened like this on Springbrook – the heavens seem to explode, elemental forces are unleashed – and a couple of hours later the sky is clear and calm again. For the rest of that Friday the services would have to be held in one of the buildings adjacent to Raphael.

The power of the wind called to the Boy. He dressed and slipped out of the house. Keeping to the massive gum trees rather than the open meadow he went the long path to the Chapel. Om still watched, then she ran. Swiftly she ran through the grass. She knew the storm would suddenly break and she would be alone with the Boy in the holy place. She jumped on to the altar just as the first huge drops of rain splattered heavily from the swollen thunderclouds. She sat bolt upright, electric with tension just as the Boy came in, running slightly, from the path that led in from the forest. He gasped when he saw her: "Om!" he exclaimed gently in a voice so old and so full of knowing, even though the knowing hadn't quite reached his head from where it lay in his heart.

"Om – you too!"

She was looking far away, beyond Time. Her eyes blazed like lapis lazuli, the lapis lazuli that Egyptians once carved their cats from for their Pharaohs. The Boy sat down in a dream on a seat in front of the altar. The fir trees, the Twelve Apostles, closed their fan like branches over the Boy and the

Cat and the rain exploded all around them, not touching them. The sky grew darker, the eerie light glowed grays and mauves and greeny yellows and the wind moaned and howled and the branches shook. The Boy stared and stared at Om – she vibrated with light, there was so much light around her that the Boy had to keep blinking to bring her into focus. There was a roll of thunder that made the earth tremble and a sword of lightning that split the heavens in two, and there, in the brilliant gap of shimmering light in the darkened sky the Boy could see the form of the Cross, like a star, and echoing with the thundering rolling clouds he heard a tremendous voice cry out of the darkness: "Abba, it is finished!"

The Boy lost consciousness. The twelve trees bowed their branches even closer, and Om came back from where she had been. Within minutes the clouds of dark and thunder were scudding across the sky and the wind died down and the rain stopped. The whole mountain seemed cleansed. Om sat very close to the Boy, breathing on to his eyelids. Slowly he sat up and the branches of the twelve great trees lifted to let him stand and pass. He walked home across the saturated meadow, went quietly in through the back door, pulled on a heavy cotton sweatshirt and climbed into bed. A strange light surrounded him and a strange peace flooded through him. He fell into a deep and dreamless sleep.

The following day he had a soaring temperature, but it was the heat from the heart that burned with love in the Heart of hearts, and not a fever. He slept fitfully through the day. Om and Ralph Cupboard kept their own vigil. Dave said he would stay at home if 'Reen wanted to go to the Easter Vigil and a frown passed over 'Reen's face. She told her husband that Dr. Jefferson had more or less insisted Patrick come too, said he had found Pat's Cat on the altar and he felt it was a symbol or something. Neither she nor Dave knew of the Boy's experience of the previous day.

"Well," said Dave, pursing his lips and closing up the newspaper he wasn't really looking at, "Pat's not fit enough to go anywhere at the moment ..." and before he could finish the sentence there was a noise at the door and he turned to see the Boy standing in what looked like sunlight, except, said Dave to 'Reen afterwards, the sun was shining from the opposite side of the house and couldn't light that particular doorway. Even the Boy's voice sounded different when he spoke and said: "I'd like to go to the Vigil tonight, and I'd like you to come too. The ground is dry again now and it will be held in the Tree Chapel. The fire that lights the candle will be my own fire, don't ask me what I mean, I am not sure that I know, but I must be there, and you too."

He turned and went back to his room. He knew he needed to spend some time with Ralph Cupboard who loved him.

"There's something different about that Boy," said 'Reen. "He sounded quite grown up you know, but oh, he looked so pale and I'm really worried."

"Don't know about pale, 'Reen," answered Dave thoughtfully, "more like, well, like moonlight, y'know, that glowing sort of light?"

When supper was ready 'Reen called the Boy who came with Ralph Cupboard bundled up in his arms. He took some orange juice. Nothing more.

They walked together over to the Chapel. Dr. Jefferson, now in his white silk cope and embroidered stole, had lit the fire and moved like a luminous figure illumined by the flickering fire flames and the moon. The night was still and clear, the Southern Cross suspended in the dense deep night blue sky above the mountain.

The words swam in and out of the Boy's mind and hearing

as he watched in awe of the shining cross-like star he was certain he had never seen before in the night sky.

Ralph Cupboard watched ... and knew the pain was Love.

"... on this most holy night ... come together in vigil and prayer ... make this new fire holy." He watched the Easter candle be lit from the fire ... "the beginning and the end, Alpha and Omega: All time belongs to Him and all the ages ... dispel our darkness."

The candle was lifted high above the altar. The Boy stared and stared at the flickering flame, and as he stared he knew the flame was his. Soundlessly he drew back from the firelight and slipped away into the night and walked softly home. Om was now waiting, she looked unreal somehow, but then everything looked unreal, the only reality was the living flame that burned in his heart. Om seemed to shimmer and flicker like a silver flame before him, and his eyes grew dim, the stars grew pale. He sat in his father's chair, staring and staring at the white star just outside his window. Never had he seen such a star ... it shimmered and moved and he saw that it was ringed with silver and was distinctly now the shape of the Cross. Slowly he withdrew his gaze and closed his eyes.

A light wind sprang up, the service was over. Two hours had passed. 'Reen and Dave had not seen their child slip away into the night and now they hurried home. They found him in the big armchair and thought he was just asleep ... But Om had gone.

With his last out breath the Boy had whispered the sound to himself of the words "Om, Om, Om," and Om had carried the Boy's soul with her on the wind.

Ralph Cupboard, when he looked up at the Easter Star outside the window, felt his heart would burst. And he sat and sat, looking up at the Star, which he knew only he could see, and he knew that the pain that he felt in his heart was ... Love.

Om Tat Sat